D1385348

The Adventures of Oliver Poons

Oliver Poons and the Bright Yellow Hat

Written by Lauryn Alyssa Wendus

Illustrated by Lois Wendus

Ribbon Star Press

For information regarding written permission, write to:

Ribbon Star Press
2842 Main Street #110
Glastonbury, CT 06033

Library of Congress Control Number: 2014919757
ISBN 978-0-9909857-6-1

Published by Ribbon Star Press, a division of Next Door Creations, LLC.
Oliver Poons and associated logos are trademarks of Next Door Creations, LLC.

The illustrations were done in watercolor.

10 9 8 7 6 5 4 3 2

Printed in Stevens Point, WI, U.S.A.
April 2015

This Book Belongs to:

....

To Oliver for his constant love and companionship,

To No Kitten Left Behind for rescuing one of many lovable cats,

To the kindness of friends and family,

And to all those who bring the world a little sunshine.

To all the children:

May Oliver Poons and his friends bring you much joy.
May he bring a smile to your face and a ray of sunshine to your day.

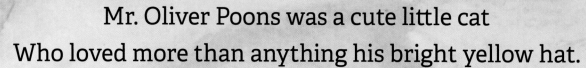

Mr. Oliver Poons was a cute little cat
Who loved more than anything his bright yellow hat.

He took it through the meadows
And to the beach.
To the tops of hills,
Wherever he could reach!

But then one day he
ran into Orange Kitty

Who told him he did
not look very pretty!

"Hats are for people,
they are not for a cat!"

"You may not think
so, but I'm telling you
that!"

"Why would you say
such a thing?"
asked Mr. Poons.

"It keeps the rain off
my nose, guards my
eyes from the sun..."

"It has so many uses
all in one!"

"Besides from it making you look like a cartoon..."

(Orange Kitty began to whisper)

"Your hat hides your ears and makes you less able to hear."

"What was that last part?"
Mr. Poons asked back.

"You see," said Orange Kitty,
"You could not hear my whisper."

"That's why hats aren't meant
for things with whiskers!"

Poons was sad he'd have to stop
wearing his hat for hearing's sake...

So he took his hat on one last trip and went to the lake!

While sitting by the shore, Mr. Poons gazed at a pile of stone,
But when he looked closely, it seemed that one moved on its own!

Mr. Poons and his hat went to see what this could be about...

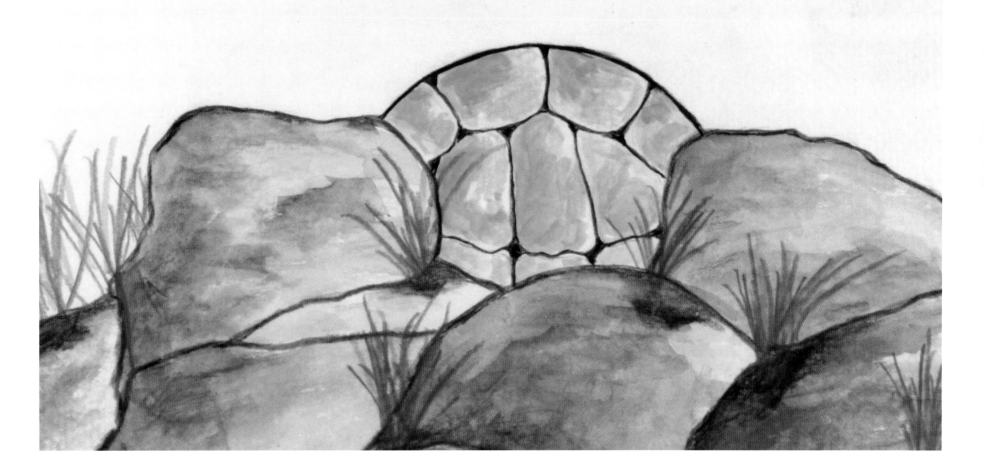

It was not a stone, but a turtle, as it turned out!

"You looked just like a stone," Poons told the turtle.

"I get that a lot. It's nice to meet you, I'm Myrtle."

"I love being a turtle because I have this nice shell,"

"It has holes for my head and for my legs," Myrtle began to tell.

"That's it!"
Poons yelled.

"That's how I can
keep my hat!"

"Thanks, Myrtle,
you've made me
one happy cat!"

Mr. Poons went in search of a sharp stick to act as a spear.
He poked two holes in his hat,
One for each ear.

Placed atop his head, his yellow hat was now just right.
He could hear just fine now, it was such a delight!

Mr. Poons could now wear his hat and hear a whisper,
And proved that hats could be for things with whiskers.

Hats can be for cats and cats can be for hats,

And it's Mr.
Poons
telling you,
"That is that!"

Who is Oliver Poons?

The character Oliver Poons is inspired by Lauryn's lovable cat, Oliver. Lauryn adopted Oliver as a kitten from the animal rescue group, *No Kitten Left Behind*, in East Hartford, CT.

Lauryn and Oliver have grown to be best friends!

See you in our next book, **Dreaming in Color!**

Ribbon Star Press